The Holly Pond Hill
Christmas
·Treasury·

Paul Kortepeter

illustrated by

Susan Wheeler

Dutton Children's Books

NEW YORK

Keep Your Christmas Merry

IMPORTANT SAFETY TIPS

Before starting any project, it's always a good idea to ask an adult for permission. They will know whether the supplies and ingredients are available. Be sure to clean up any messes you make. A good cleaner-upper is always appreciated.

1. If you plan to do any cooking, make sure an adult is in the house.
2. Wash your hands before you prepare food so that you don't add any germs to the ingredients.
3. Ask for help if a recipe calls for a blender, food processor, stove, or oven. Whenever you work at the stove, keep handles of pots and pans turned inward so there is no danger of knocking them off.
4. Never use a sharp knife or scissors without the help of an adult. When possible, use safety scissors.
5. Be especially careful when using a hot-glue gun. The tip is very hot and can burn skin easily.

Christmas is the happiest season of all. Be safe, not sorry!

Text copyright © 2003 by Paul Kortepeter
Illustrations copyright © 2003 by Susan Wheeler
Licensed by i Licensing℠, Bloomington, IN 47402
All rights reserved.

Scripture taken from the Holy Bible, New International Version. Copyright © 1973, 1978, 1984
International Bible Society. Used by permission of Zondervan Bible Publishers.

"A Call for Snow," "Letter to Santa," and "The True Gift," by Paul Kortepeter. From
Holly Pond Hill®: A Child's Book of Christmas, Dutton Children's Books. Text copyright © 2002 by Paul Kortepeter.

Published in the United States by Dutton Children's Books,
a division of Penguin Young Readers Group
345 Hudson Street, New York, New York 10014
www.penguinputnam.com

Music engraved by Robert Sherwin
Manufactured in China • First Edition
ISBN 0-525-46156-6
1 3 5 7 9 10 8 6 4 2

The publisher has made every reasonable effort to ensure that the recipes and activities in this book are safe
when carried out as instructed but assumes no responsibility for any damage or injury caused
or sustained while performing the activities in this book.

The Boxwood Family

Edmund and Victoria Rose

Emily

Oliver

Violet

Contents

Introduction

Snow

Song

Sweets

Surprises

Favorite Things

This is the Boxwood family out for a winter stroll. As you can see from the happiness in their faces, Christmas is on its way! Christmas happens to be the favorite time of the year for all the woodland creatures of Holly Pond Hill.

The bunny in the purple coat is Emily. Her favorite part of Christmas is the pretty music, especially the suite from *The Nutcracker* ballet. She whirls and twirls about the house in a pink tutu just like the Sugarplum Fairy. Once Emily went crashing into the Christmas tree and came spinning out again covered in tinsel.

The two adult rabbits are Edmund and Victoria Rose Boxwood. As with nearly all adults, their favorite part of Christmas is seeing happiness sparkle in the eyes of children. They also enjoy chatting with friends for endless hours at Christmas parties. Emily finds it truly amazing how long her parents can talk

and talk and talk without ever jumping up to play or run around.

The bunny in blue is Oliver. His favorite part of Christmas, without a doubt, is eating. He can gobble up a tray of Christmas cookies, a whole gingerbread house, and a pumpkin pie and still ask his mother "What's for dessert?" His nose is so sensitive, he can smell cherry pie baking before Victoria Rose even puts it in the oven.

Baby Violet, in the sled, loves the lights and the decorations and the excitement all around her. She loves the stockings by the fireplace, sleigh rides in the snow, toy shop windows, and little licks of her sister's candy cane.

A book of ten thousand pages or more could probably be filled with all of *your* favorite things about Christmas. But that's not the end of it, oh no! Every year you will be discovering new favorites to add to the old. Someday you might find bread pudding on your list. Or a brass band playing "Silver Bells" on a city sidewalk. Or Christmas dinner by candlelight. The possibilities are endless! Your book of Christmas favorites might be so heavy you would need a reindeer to pull it. Since you probably don't have a reindeer, you can start with this kid-sized book, full of fun and favorites from the rabbits of Holly Pond Hill.

There are ideas in this treasury for every day of the holiday season. You'll find stories and poems to read, carols to sing, recipes to try, and ideas for special gifts you can make with your own hands for the people you love.

Where should you begin? Why not sit down with your whole family on a winter's night and read this treasury together? As you read, you can decide which activities you'd like to do to count down the days before Christmas. You might decide to whip up a batch of gingerbread bunnies on one day and arrange a caroling party the next. Mark the calendar and off you go . . . it will be Christmas before you know it!

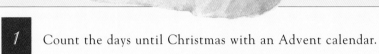

December

Make It a Tradition

Is there something you love about Christmas? Try to do the same wonderful things year after year, and they will become cherished traditions. Families draw closer when they celebrate traditions together. Remember—the small touches can be just as special as the big events. Here are 25 suggestions, one for each day leading up to Christmas.

1   Count the days until Christmas with an Advent calendar.

2   Pick out a Christmas tree at a tree lot or a tree farm.

3   String popcorn and cranberry garlands for the Christmas tree.

4   Borrow holiday books from the public library.
See the list of classic stories on page 13.

5   Read the legends about Saint Nicholas, Bishop of Myra.
Tonight, leave your shoes outside your bedroom door.

6   SAINT NICHOLAS' DAY
Eat the fruit, nuts, and chocolate you find in your shoes.

7   Record a holiday message on your answering machine.

8   Send homemade Christmas pictures to your grandparents.

9   Bundle up and take a long walk with someone special.
Think of all the ways the winter world is different from summer.

10   Set up a crèche scene, but leave the manger empty.

11   Wire a wreath to the bumper of your family's automobile.

12   Make or buy one new ornament for the tree
that reminds you of the year gone by.

13	Take a hot bubble bath and use the suds to give yourself Santa's white hair and beard.
14	Learn a Christmas poem by heart to recite to friends and neighbors.
15	Make a batch of sugar cookies or gingerbread, using Christmas cookie cutters. Tie them in bundles to deliver to elderly neighbors.
16	Attend a *Las Posadas* celebration near you, or learn the story of Hanukkah and play with a dreidel.
17	Go caroling in your neighborhood or at a nursing home. Eat hot chili afterward.
18	Write love notes to your family, roll them into scrolls, and tie them to the tree with ribbons. No peeking till Christmas Day!
19	Using ribbon, hang pieces of toast or unsalted pretzels from the branches of a tree as a gift to the birds.
20	Call your relatives long-distance to wish them Merry Christmas.
21	Watch a Christmas movie with your family while sipping hot chocolate and munching on fresh popcorn.
22	Spend the day making and wrapping presents. Spend the night camping under the Christmas tree.
23	Read the Christmas story from the Gospel of Luke or "The Night Before Christmas" by Clement Clarke Moore.
24	Enjoy the Christmas Eve candlelight service at church or stay up for midnight mass.
25	CHRISTMAS DAY! Place baby Jesus in the crèche manger. Play charades with your family after all the gifts have been opened.

Classic Christmas Stories and Poems

Here are some books that make Christmas such a special time for reading. Picture books are available for most of the titles below:

The Fir Tree
HANS CHRISTIAN ANDERSEN

The Little Match Girl
HANS CHRISTIAN ANDERSEN

A Christmas Carol
CHARLES DICKENS

How the Grinch Stole Christmas
DR. SEUSS

The Gift of the Magi
O. HENRY

The Baker's Dozen: A Saint Nicholas Tale
AARON SHEPARD

The Selfish Giant
OSCAR WILDE

The Nutcracker
E. T. A. HOFFMANN

Shoemaker Martin
LEO TOLSTOY

The Night Before Christmas
CLEMENT CLARKE MOORE

Stopping by Woods on a Snowy Evening
ROBERT FROST

The Lamb
WILLIAM BLAKE

Christmas Everywhere
PHILLIP BROOKS

The Shepherds Had an Angel
CHRISTINA ROSSETTI

SusanWheeler

Snow

SNOW SONG

How joyous is this time of year,
When hearts are bright
With Christmas cheer.
Join we our hands about the tree
And sing a Yuletide melody.

Our voices dance from hill to hill
Where curls of smoke rise high and still,
And frosted windows warmly glow,
Lighting the lace of falling snow.

A CALL FOR SNOW

Snow harder! Snow more!
Snow blizzards galore!
I can't get enough
Of this fluffy white stuff!
Snow! Snow! Snow!
Snow a ton! Snow a heap!
Snow ten feet deep!
I wouldn't cry
If it snowed till July.
Snow! Snow! Snow!

The First Snowflake

Emily and Oliver Boxwood were sitting side by side on the old stone wall in front of their house. They had heard the weather report from a passing flock of redbirds. "Snowstorm!" squawked the birds. "Two feet and not an inch less!" Now Emily and Oliver were waiting for the snow.

"See any flakes yet?" asked Oliver.

"Not yet," Emily said, glancing at the gray sky.

"See any flakes?" asked Oliver.

"I just *said* not *yet*," Emily answered sharply.

"Okay, *okay*," said Oliver. "I won't ask again for a long time."

With every passing minute, the wall felt colder. Oh, how their bottoms ached! The wind blustered through their fur, and every little breath came out of their noses in a frozen puff.

"See any flakes?" asked Oliver again.

Emily sighed loudly. "Why don't you make up a snow poem," she suggested. "That might help the snow along."

Oliver cleared his throat. "I don't mind if I do."

Where are you, Snow,
On this cold, nippy day?
The trees are all brown
And the sky is all gray.
Without some white soon,
I'll have no heart to play.
So come on, Snow—SNOW!
Fall on my head and cover my toes.
Fill up my ears and tickle my nose.
Come on, Snow, SNOW!

The two rabbits stared intently at the sky. For at least a minute, nothing happened. Then a single snowflake came spinning out of the gray above.

"I don't believe it!" Oliver shouted. "My poem worked!"

He hopped off the fence and went chasing after the flake, his tongue stretched out. Emily came bounding after him.

"No, Oliver, don't!" she cried. "Don't eat the first snowflake!" She caught it on her mitten. "Each one is a work of art. Don't you know that no two snowflakes are exactly alike? If you lick this flake, the world will never again see such beauty."

Oliver rolled his eyes. Emily could be so dramatic. But he had to admit that it *was* a beautiful flake. It had six pointy sides and looked like a lacy star. "I'm sorry that I tried to lick it," he said contritely. At that moment, a second flake twirled past his face. With a bounce, he raced off, licking at the wind.

"Stop, Oliver, stop!" shouted Emily, dashing along beside him.

"What now?!" His mouth was poised under the flake, just waiting for it to land. "Can't I eat the second snowflake at least?"

"But this snowflake is just as lovely as the first." Emily jumped up and rescued it from the pink tongue below. "The answer is no, no, no!"

By this time, flakes were starting to fall all around them. They fell in twos and threes, in fours and fives, and finally they tumbled out of the sky in buckets and bushels. It seemed that the whole world had turned white in an instant. The white gathered on the ground, on the stone wall, and in the trees.

Emily and Oliver stood side by side in the middle of the snowstorm, completely amazed by the thick curtain of white.

"I don't suppose we'd want to dance around," Oliver said wistfully. "We wouldn't want to crush these pretty snowflakes, right?"

"Right," said Emily.

"And we wouldn't want to do cartwheels either?"

"No," said Emily, with less certainty in her voice.

Oliver let out a heavy sigh. "I suppose snow angels are a bad idea, too?"

Emily looked longingly at the snow, which was beginning to heap up in every direction. "Well, snow angels . . . that's different. Isn't that what snow is for?"

"You can't have a snow angel without snow, that's the truth!"

Emily and Oliver immediately flopped on their backs and fanned their arms and legs. Oh, how soft and feathery the fresh snow felt! And, of course, they opened their mouths and ate every snowflake that landed on their tongues. And why not? Wasn't snow also made for this?

Maple Slush

When the world outdoors is covered in frosty white, it looks like a giant dish of vanilla ice cream. Vanilla is fine, as far as it goes, but vanilla and maple are better yet! This delicious recipe comes from the maple syrup–producing regions of New England and Canada. You'll have to wait for a few inches of fresh snow to fall, so be sure to keep these ingredients on hand. Maple slush goes well with short-bread cookies and a crackling fire.

1 cup whole milk

1/2 cup real maple syrup

1 teaspoon vanilla extract

Clean, fresh snow

❊ Stir milk, maple syrup, and vanilla together in a large bowl.

❊ Carry bowl outside. With a large spoon, scoop snow into bowl. Stir enough snow into the other ingredients to absorb them fully.

❊ Go back inside and scoop slush into smaller bowls.

Splatter Snow

Imagine that the snow in your backyard is a huge blank sheet of paper. It's time to paint! This activity works best on a cold, sunny day.

❊ Squeeze various food colors into containers of cold water. Use enough dye to yield a strong color. To keep colors bright, avoid mixing them.

❊ Fill spray bottles and squirt guns with colored water. You may also use open jars and paintbrushes.

❊ Spray a patch of snow with crisscrossing spots and spatters of color. Fling the colors off the paintbrushes. (Be careful not to spill food coloring on your clothes—it can stain.)

❊ After spraying and spattering, step back to view your masterpiece. If it's too beautiful to just melt away, make sure you take a picture!

Snow-White Frosting

This firm frosting decorates Christmas treats almost as well as real snow.

    1 cup shortening

    1 1/2 teaspoons vanilla extract

    1/2 teaspoon lemon, peppermint, or
        butterscotch extract

    4 1/2 cups powdered sugar

    3 to 4 tablespoons milk

❊ Combine shortening and extracts in a large mixing bowl and beat with an electric mixer (medium setting) for about 30 seconds.

❊ Gradually add half of the powdered sugar, beating continuously.

❊ Add 2 tablespoons of milk.

❊ Slowly add the remainder of sugar and milk until the frosting is firm and easy to spread.

Snowy Trees

If you get a sugar-cone craving in the middle of winter, here is a way to enjoy these crispy treats without the chill of ice cream! These cones look like snow-covered trees and can be used to create winter scenes.

❊ Turn sugar cones upside down and place them one by one in a muffin tin.

❊ Spread white frosting over each cone until completely covered.

❊ Decorate your snowy trees with gold and silver candy balls or with any small holiday candy.

Marshmallow and Crispy-Rice Snowmen

These crisp, chewy treats are fast becoming a Yuletide favorite.

3 tablespoons butter
4 cups mini-marshmallows
1 teaspoon vanilla extract
4 cups crisped rice cereal
Marshmallow Fluff™
Decorating ingredients: raisins or
  chocolate chips, pretzel sticks, candy corn

❋ In a large saucepan, melt butter over low heat. Add marshmallows and vanilla. Stir constantly until marshmallows are gooey and melted.

❋ Add the crisped rice cereal and stir until the cereal is coated. Allow coated cereal to cool for approximately 10 minutes.

❋ Line a cookie sheet with wax paper.

❋ Grease hands with butter. When the cereal handles easily but is still warm, shape into balls. Make larger balls for the snowman bodies and smaller balls for the heads, then press together. If necessary, use a small amount of Marshmallow Fluff to form a stronger bond.

❋ Decorate snowmen with raisins and chocolate chips for eyes, mouth, and buttons; pretzel sticks for arms; and candy corn for nose. Use dabs of Marshmallow Fluff to improve the sticking power of your decorations.

❋ Place in refrigerator to make firm before serving.

Once There Was a Snowman

Once there was a snowman
Who stood outside the door.
He wished that he could come inside
And run about the floor.
He wished that he could warm himself
Beside the fire, so red.
He wished that he could climb
Upon the big white bed.

So he called to the North Wind,
"Come and help me, pray,
For I'm completely frozen
Standing out here all day."
So the North Wind came along
And blew him in the door.
And now there's nothing left of him
But a puddle on the floor!

ANONYMOUS

Susan
Wheeler

Glad tidings we bring
To you and your kin
Glad tidings of Christmas
And a happy New Year!

Susan Wheeler

John 5:24

Song

WELCOME HERE!

Welcome here, welcome here,
All be alive and be of good cheer.

I made a loaf that's cooling there,
With my neighbors I will share.
Come, all ye people, hear me sing
A song of friendly welcoming.

I've got a pie all baked complete,
Pudding, too, that's very sweet.
Chestnuts are roasting, join us here
While we dance and make good cheer.

I've got a log that's burning hot,
Toddy's bubbling in the pot.
Come in, ye people, where it's warm,
The wind blows sharp and it may storm.

Welcome here, welcome here,
All be alive and be of good cheer.

TRADITIONAL SHAKER POEM

AN OLD CHRISTMAS GREETING

Sing Hey! Sing Hey!
For Christmas Day,
Twine mistletoe and holly;
For friendship grows
In winter snows,
And so let's all be jolly.

ANONYMOUS

Joy to the World

A crackling fire. A steaming mug of chocolate. Carols out in the snow. Could there be anything better? Oliver Boxwood thought that these nights under the starry winter sky were the best nights of all to be alive.

I'm so happy I could burst, he thought as he warmed his toes. The marshmallow he was toasting over the fire *did* burst but not from happiness. It burst into flames, and Oliver hastily blew them out. He was too happy to feel the slightest irritation. With a look of bliss on his face, he ate the blackened goo.

"Can we sing 'Joy to the World'?" he asked.

"We just finished singing 'Joy to the World,' dear," said Victoria Rose, his mother.

"Oh," Oliver said. "Maybe that's why I thought of it." He had obviously been too focused on his marshmallow and his own happiness to notice the song. "Well, let's keep singing. Any Christmas carol will do. They're all happy, and I'm happy, too."

"Not true!" Emily piped up.

"Yes, I am!" Oliver squeaked. He was shocked that anyone would question how he felt inside.

"No, I meant I know a sad Christmas carol," Emily said. "It goes like this." Emily started singing plaintively:

> *Once in Royal David's city*
> *Stood a lowly cattle shed,*
> *Where a mother laid her baby*
> *In a manger for His bed:*
> *Mary was that mother mild,*
> *Jesus Christ her little child.*

> *He came down to earth from heaven,*
> *Who is God and Lord of all,*
> *And His shelter was a stable,*
> *And His cradle was a stall;*
> *With the poor, and mean, and lowly*
> *Lived on earth our Savior Holy.*

Oliver felt genuinely distressed that there could be a sad carol in the world. It seemed as if a star had fallen, dimming the winter sky. Even the fire seemed to shrink into itself and lose its warmth. Oliver felt chilled for the first time that night. While he sat there shivering, Oliver heard a brass band playing far off in the village. He could barely hear the music, but he knew that it was a familiar tune. Suddenly the words sprang into his head, and he sang out:

> *Ding dong! Merrily on high,*
> *In heav'n the bells are ringing!*

"Now that's a happy tune," he said. "Oh, there's lots more happy carols than sad ones. What about the one with the mountains echoing joyous strains? And bells ringing on bobtail, laughing all the way? And the love and joy parts in that song about the three ships wassailing or something. See what I mean?"

"Even Emily's sad carol has a happy ending," said Mama gently. "Yes, it must have been a hard thing to bring a baby into the world like that, in a stable far from home. But the Christmas story ends with rejoicing." And Victoria Rose sang the last verse:

Not in that poor lowly stable,
With the oxen standing by,
We shall see Him; but in heaven,
Set at God's right hand on high;
When like stars His children crowned
All in white shall wait around.

Oliver's face grew blissfully bright. "I love songs like that—the ones that start out sad! They're even happier than the happy ones."

"What about 'In the Bleak Midwinter'?" Emily asked. "Now *that* is a sad carol. It goes like this—"

"Emily, dear," her mother interrupted, "what if we sing a song everyone knows, like 'Deck the Halls'?"

And so the group sang their *fa la las* with gusto, with Oliver's voice the loudest of all. The heavens were bright again, and the fire was warm. There was no doubt in his mind that these nights under the starry winter sky were the best nights of all to be alive.

Joy to the World

ISAAC WATTS, 1719

GEORGE F. HANDEL, 1742
ARR. BY LOWELL MASON, 1830

Joy to the world! The Lord is come; Let earth re-

ceive her King; _____ Let ev - 'ry heart _____ pre-

pare Him room, _____ And heav'n and na - ture sing, And

heav'n and na - ture sing, And heav'n, And heav'n _____ and na - ture sing.

Share a Song of Christmas

You simply must go caroling! What fun it is to go sliding down a frosty lane, sharing Christmas joy with friends and neighbors. Gather together a group of kids and adults and practice several Christmas carols until everyone has mastered the tunes. Then plan a route in your neighborhood (or in a residential home for seniors) and stop at houses that are decked out for Christmas.

Deck the Halls

TRADITIONAL

OLD WELSH AIR

Deck the halls with boughs of hol - ly, Fa la la la la, la la la la.

'Tis the sea - son to be jol - ly, Fa la la la la, la la la la.

Don we now our gay ap - par - el, Fa la, la la, la la la.

Troll the an - cient Yule - tide car - ol, Fa la la la la, la la la la.

2.
See the blazing yule before us,
Fa la la la la, la la la la.
Strike the harp and join the chorus,
Fa la la la la, la la la la.
Follow me in merry measure,
Fa la, la la, la la la.
While I sing of Yuletide treasure,
Fa la la la la, la la la la!

3.
Fast away the old year passes,
Fa la la la la, la la la la.
Hail the new, ye lads and lasses,
Fa la la la la, la la la la.
Sing we joyous all together,
Fa la, la la, la la la.
Heedless of the wind and weather,
Fa la la la la, la la la la!

Hark! The Herald Angels Sing

CHARLES WESLEY, 1739

FELIX MENDELSSOHN, 1840
ARR. BY W. H. CUMMINGS, 1855

Hark! The her-ald an-gels sing, "Glo-ry to the new-born King! Peace on earth, and mer-cy mild, God and sin-ners re-con-ciled." Joy-ful, all ye na-tions rise, Join the tri-umph of the skies; With th'an-gel-ic host pro-claim, "Christ is born in

REFRAIN

Beth-le-hem." Hark! The her-ald an-gels sing, "Glo-ry to the new-born King!"

2.
Christ, by highest heav'n adored;
Christ, the everlasting Lord;
Late in time behold Him come,
Offspring of the favored one,
Veiled in flesh, the Godhead see;
Hail th'incarnate Deity
Pleased, as man with men to dwell,
Jesus, our Immanuel!

REFRAIN

3.
Hail! The heav'n born Prince of Peace!
Hail! The Son of Righteousness!
Light and life to all He brings,
Ris'n with healing in His wings.
Mild He lays His glory by,
Born that man no more may die;
Born to raise the sons of earth,
Born to give them second birth.

REFRAIN

O Christmas Tree

TRADITIONAL

O Christ-mas tree, O Christ-mas tree, Thy leaves are so un - chang - ing. O Christ-mas tree, O

Christ-mas tree, Thy leaves are so un - chang - ing. Not on - ly green when sum-mer's here, But

al - so when 'tis cold and drear. O Christ-mas tree, O Christ-mas tree, Thy leaves are so un - chang - ing.

2.

O Christmas tree, O Christmas tree,
  You fill our hearts with gaiety.
O Christmas tree, O Christmas tree,
  You fill our hearts with gaiety.
On Christmas Day you stand so tall,
  Affording joy to one and all.
O Christmas tree, O Christmas tree,
  You fill our hearts with gaiety.

3.

O Christmas Tree, O Christmas Tree,
  How faithful are thy branches!
O Christmas Tree, O Christmas Tree,
  How faithful are thy branches!
O Christmas Tree, O Christmas Tree,
  Green not alone in summertime,
  But in the winter's frost and rime;
O Christmas Tree, O Christmas Tree,
  How faithful are thy branches.

We Wish You a Merry Christmas

TRADITIONAL

OLD ENGLISH OR SCOTTISH AIR
ARR. BY NICK NICHOLSON

We wish you a Mer-ry Christ-mas, We wish you a Mer-ry Christ-mas, We

REFRAIN

wish you a Mer-ry Christ-mas And a Hap-py New Year! Good tid-ings we bring to

you and your kin; Good tid-ings for Christ-mas And a Hap-py New Year!

2.

Now bring us some figgy pudding,
Now bring us some figgy pudding,
Now bring us some figgy pudding,
    And bring it out here.

REFRAIN

3.

We won't go until we get some,
We won't go until we get some,
We won't go until we get some,
    So bring some out here.

REFRAIN

After-Caroling Treats

Now comes the cozy part of caroling. Unless you've been treated to hot drinks along the way, the best ending to an evening outdoors is beside a crackling fire with a mug of something hot. Chicken soup or hot chocolate never tasted so good! Better yet, prepare a pot of chili at the beginning of the day and treat your fellow carolers to a meal.

Hot Cocoa with Peppermint

The perfect warmer-upper after an evening of caroling

1/4 cup unsweetened cocoa powder

1/4 cup sugar

1 quart milk

Peppermint sticks or candy canes

❊ In a small saucepan, combine cocoa, sugar, and 1 cup of milk. Stir well.

❊ Stir in remaining milk, using a whisk or eggbeater to make sure it is well blended.

❊ Simmer over low heat. Place a peppermint stick or a small candy cane into each mug you serve.

❊ Makes 4 servings.

Slow-Cookin' Chili

It's a cinch to throw this chili together the morning of your caroling party so it can cook all day. (Parental help is a must!)

1 pound ground turkey or hamburger

1 28 oz.-can crushed tomatoes, undrained

1 15 oz.-can each of great northern beans, kidney beans, and black beans

1 10 oz.-can enchilada sauce

1 8 oz.-can tomato sauce

1 4.5 oz.-can chopped green chilies

1 green bell pepper, seeded and chopped

1 cup chopped onion

2 to 3 teaspoons chili powder

1 teaspoon ground cumin

Optional toppings: shredded cheddar cheese, sour cream, finely chopped onion

❊ Brown ground turkey or hamburger in skillet and drain.

❊ Place meat and all other ingredients in a slow cooker (Crock-Pot). Mix well.

❊ Cover and cook on low for 9 hours or until pepper and onion are tender.

❊ Serve chili with shredded cheese, sour cream, and minced raw onions, if desired.

Sweets

THE CHRISTMAS PUDDING

Into the basin put the plums,
Stirabout, stirabout, stirabout!

Next the good white flour comes,
Stirabout, stirabout, stirabout!

Sugar and peel and eggs and spice,
Stirabout, stirabout, stirabout!

Mix them and fix them and cook them twice,
Stirabout, stirabout, stirabout!

TRADITIONAL

LETTER TO SANTA

Dear Santa,
We baked these cookies
just for you.
Please give some to your
reindeer, too.
We made them from scratch,
but we must confess
we left the kitchen an awful mess.
Enjoy the milk and stay to eat,
and Mama says
please wipe your feet.

Sweet Tooth

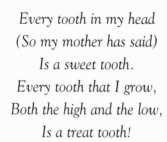

Every tooth in my head
(So my mother has said)
Is a sweet tooth.
Every tooth that I grow,
Both the high and the low,
Is a treat tooth!

For birthdays, I've a cake tooth.
For hot days, I've a shake tooth.
I've a candy tooth for Hallowe'ens
And a choc'late tooth for Valenteens.

For Christmas, full of cookies and pies,
My teeth get sweeter and so do my eyes.
My nose smells mince a mile away,
My tongue tastes tarts all night and day.

On Christmas, I eat with all my might,
But I always save room for one more bite.
I beg my mom, "Please don't stop baking!
My poor sweet teeth are all a-shaking!"

Now you see that it's true,
And no use to argue,
I've a sweet tooth.
Every tooth in my mouth,
From the north to the south,
Is a treat tooth.

OLIVER BOXWOOD

Cookies for Christmas

A true Christmas cookie is no ordinary cookie—it can only be found during the holiday season.
No matter how fancy you make oatmeal or peanut-butter cookies, they never quite have
the magic of once-a-year gingerbread or Christmas tea cakes.

Christmas Tea Cakes

These yummy cookies look like miniature snowballs.

1/2 cup (1 stick) softened butter

2 tablespoons granulated sugar

1 cup all-purpose flour

1 cup pecans, chopped fine

1 teaspoon vanilla

Confectioners' sugar for rolling

❋ Preheat oven to 300° F.

❋ Cream softened butter in a medium bowl.
Add sugar gradually and beat together.

❋ Stir in flour, pecans, and vanilla.

❋ Roll dough into one-inch balls.

❋ Place dough balls on an ungreased cookie
sheet and bake for 30 minutes.

❋ While tea cakes are still warm, roll in
confectioners' sugar until coated white.

Gingerbread Bunnies

Go ahead—nibble on the ears first!

1/2 cup (1 stick) softened butter

1/2 cup light brown sugar

1 egg

3/4 cup molasses

3 cups flour

1/4 teaspoon salt

1/2 teaspoon baking soda

1 teaspoon each ground ginger and cinnamon

1/2 teaspoon each ground cloves and ground nutmeg

Raisins, currants, and icing for decoration

❋ Preheat oven to 350° F.

❋ Beat butter and brown sugar together until fluffy.
Add the egg and molasses, and mix well.

❋ In another bowl, mix together the flour, salt,
baking soda, ginger, cinnamon, cloves, and nutmeg.
Slowly stir into butter mixture. Mix until combined.

❋ Cover bowl and chill for 4 hours.

❋ On a well-floured surface, roll out dough until it's
about 1/4-inch thick, and cut with cookie cutters.
Press raisins or currants into bunny heads to make
eyes and onto bunny bodies to make buttons.

❋ Place cookies on a greased cookie sheet and
bake for 8 minutes.

❋ When cookies are completely cool, decorate
them with icing.

Chocolate Chippers for Santa

These thick and yummy cookies are like the kind you buy in bakeshops. Don't leave too many out for Santa or his tummy might be too round to easily get back up the chimney.

12 tablespoons (1 1/2 sticks) butter, melted and
    cooled (but still warm)
1 cup dark brown sugar
1/2 cup granulated sugar
1 large egg plus 1 egg yolk
2 teaspoons vanilla extract
2 1/8 cups (2 cups + 2 tablespoons) all-purpose flour
1/2 teaspoon baking soda
1/4 teaspoon salt
2 cups dark chocolate chips or holiday M&Ms™
Parchment paper

✳ Preheat oven to 325° F.
✳ Using an electric mixer, beat butter and sugars until mixed thoroughly. Stir in egg, extra yolk, and vanilla extract.
✳ Add flour, baking soda, and salt, stirring until just mixed. Fold in chocolate chips or M&Ms.
✳ Shape into balls of dough, using approximately 1/4 cup for each ball.
✳ Place dough onto cookie sheets lined with parchment paper.
✳ Bake cookies for 15 to 18 minutes or until golden brown. Cool on the cookie sheets.

Sugar Cookies

This is the perfect recipe for Christmas cookie cutters. Be sure to chill the dough for several hours or overnight.

1/4 cup butter
3/4 cup sugar
1 egg
1 teaspoon vanilla
1 tablespoon milk
1 1/2 cups flour
1/8 teaspoon salt
1/4 teaspoon baking powder
Cookie decorations:
    sugar sprinkles, colored frosting, silver balls

✳ In a medium bowl, cream butter. Gradually add sugar, beating until fluffy.
✳ Add egg, vanilla, and milk and beat thoroughly.
✳ Mix flour, salt, and baking powder together in a separate bowl. Add dry ingredients to wet ingredients and stir well.
✳ Divide dough in half. Cover. Chill for 3 hours.
✳ Preheat oven to 350° F.
✳ On a lightly floured surface, roll half the dough 1/4 inch thick.
✳ Cut dough into desired shapes with cookie cutters. When first half is finished, roll and cut the second half.
✳ Place dough shapes on ungreased cookie sheet and bake 8-10 minutes or until lightly browned.
✳ Cool on rack. When completely cool, decorate cookies with frosting, colored sprinkles, and silver balls.

Candy Crafts

Candy and crafts—what a delicious combination!
You can track down most supplies listed here at craft and notion stores.

Reindeer Candy Canes

These cuties can hang from the tree with a red ribbon or be used as a stir stick for a mug of hot cocoa.

Unwrapped candy canes

Brown pipe cleaners

Superglue or glue gun

Miniature (6mm) craft eyes, two for each reindeer

Miniature red pom-poms

Narrow red or green ribbon

✳ The brown pipe cleaners are the reindeers' antlers. Twist pipe cleaner under the neck of the candy cane and twist it once on top. Bend the wire on both sides into Z shapes, trimming the ends with scissors to the desired length.

✳ Glue two eyes and a red pom-pom for the nose to the curve of each candy cane, forming the face. (Caution: Glue guns are hot—ask an adult to help.)

✳ Tie a short length of ribbon in a bow one inch below the crook of the candy cane.

Candy Wreaths

You can decorate your home with these wreaths and share the candy with friends after Christmas.

Sturdy cardboard paper plates

Scissors or craft knife

Green tempera paint

White glue or glue gun

Variety of wrapped candies

Small pinecones (optional)

Red bows and ribbons

✳ Using sturdy cardboard plates, cut out a circle in the center of each. (Adults may use a craft knife.)

✳ Paint each plate a solid coating of green. Allow to dry.

✳ Glue candies and pinecones to the wreath. Be creative, but please be careful if you use a hot-glue gun!

✳ Hang wreaths with red bows and ribbons.

Gumdrop Trees

Don't wait till Christmas to eat your gumdrop tree, or it will be too hard and chewy!

Round toothpicks

Green gumdrops

Styrofoam craft cones

Assorted gummy bears

Optional: white icing, candy sprinkles

❊ Snap toothpicks in half. Stick the pointed ends of the toothpicks into the green gumdrops and the broken ends into the Styrofoam. Be careful to avoid splinters!

❊ Cover the cone with green gumdrops, leaving small spaces here and there for a rainbow assortment of gummy bears.

❊ Stick toothpicks into gummy bears and fill in the gaps of your tree.

❊ White icing can be drizzled on the treetops to look like snow. Add candy sprinkles if desired.

Surprises

THE JOY OF GIVING

Somehow, not only for Christmas
But all the long year through,
The joy that you give to others
Is the joy that comes back to you;
And the more you spend in blessing
The poor and lonely and sad,
The more of your heart's possessing
Returns to make you glad.

JOHN GREENLEAF WHITTIER

THE TRUE GIFT

Under the ribbon,
Under the bow,
Inside the box
Is a gift, you know.
But in my smile
And in my eyes
And in my heart
The true gift lies.
That gift, my dear,
Is a love steadfast—
So deep, so high
So strong, so vast.

Go to Sleep, Brother

*This poem is best read aloud with
two voices, a BOY and a GIRL.*

Sister, O sister, do you hear that noise?
It sounds like the whoosh of a sleigh full of toys!

Go to sleep, brother, that's only the breeze
Blowing in through the cracks and making me freeze.

But sister, O sister, hear that noise on the roof?
It sounds like the click of a reindeer's small hoof!

Go to sleep, brother—it's sleet that you hear
Clicking and clacking and sounding like deer.

Dear sister, sweet sister, please listen with care.
I hear jolly laughter and footsteps up there!

Go to sleep, brother—no more fabrications.
It's just your poor nerves and some wild cogitations.

What, sister? What, sister? What did you say?
Now surely you hear the bells of a sleigh.

Don't bother me, brother! Not one more peep!
Santa won't come till you're fast asleep.

Sister, you're right and I'm wrong, I suppose. *yawn*
I guess it won't hurt if I let myself doze . . . *snore*

Now brother, dear brother, you're talking some sense.
Snooze hard on your pillow without the suspense.

I'm nine and I'm old, and I'm wiser than you.
I'm smart and I'm humble—I know just what to do.

HO! HO! HO!

Hey, brother, wake up! I think you were right!
Oh, how can you sleep on a night like tonight?

The Christmas Story

LUKE 2:1–20

*This passage from the Gospel of Luke is one of the most loved in the entire Bible.
And no wonder! It tells the story of a miraculous birth. It tells of a king born in the lowliest
of circumstances—a stable filled with animals—who brings salvation to the world.
Here is the Christ who gives his name to the word Christmas.*

In those days Caesar Augustus issued a decree that a census* should be taken of the entire Roman world. . . . And everyone went to his own town to register.

So Joseph also went up from the town of Nazareth in Galilee to Judea, to Bethlehem, the town of David, because he belonged to the house and line of David. He went there to register with Mary, who was pledged to be married to him and was expecting a child. While they were there, the time came for the baby to be born, and she gave birth to her firstborn, a son. She wrapped him in cloths and placed him in a manger, because there was no room for them in the inn.

And there were shepherds living out in the fields nearby, keeping watch over their flocks at night. An angel of the Lord appeared to them, and the glory of the Lord shone around them, and they were terrified. But the angel said to them, "Do not be afraid. I bring you good news of great joy that will be for all the people. Today in the town of David a Savior has been born to you: You will find a baby wrapped in cloths and lying in a manger."

Suddenly a great company of the heavenly host appeared with the angel, praising God and saying, "Glory to God in the highest, and on earth peace to men on whom his favor rests."

When the angels had left them and gone into heaven, the shepherds said to one another, "Let's go to Bethlehem and see this thing that has happened, which the Lord has told us about."

So they hurried off and found Mary and Joseph, and the baby, who was lying in the manger. When they had seen him, they spread the word concerning what had been told them about this child, and all who heard it were amazed at what the shepherds said to them. But Mary treasured up all these things and pondered them in her heart.

The shepherds returned, glorifying and praising God for all the things they had heard and seen, which were just as they had been told.

* A counting of all the people in the land

Long, Long Ago

Winds through the olive trees
Softly did blow,
Round little Bethlehem
Long, long ago.

Sheep on the hillside lay
Whiter than snow;
Shepherds were watching them,
Long, long ago.

Then from the happy sky,
Angels bent low,
Singing their songs of joy,
Long, long ago.

For in a manger bed,
Cradled we know,
Christ came to Bethlehem,
Long, long ago.

ANONYMOUS

Handmade by You

Homemade gifts are often the most special. In this busy season—when everyone is dashing from store to store—it is such a welcome surprise to find something homemade under the tree. "What a clever idea!" people will exclaim. Here are a few favorite ideas from the Boxwood family.

Handmade Picture Frame

Make a gift of your smiling face!

A photo of yourself

Tagboard or cardboard

Ruler

Pencil

Scissors

Clear tape

Glue

Decorations: Christmas candy, stickers, markers, buttons, seashells, glitter, felt, etc.

Yarn

❊ Pick out the photo you want to frame.

❊ Lay the photo down on the tagboard. Using your ruler, measure two inches around every side of the photo and draw straight lines.

❊ Cut out the rectangle.

❊ Center the photo in the rectangle; trace around it.

❊ Cut along the inside of the tracing to provide an overlap of tagboard with which to frame the photo.

❊ Decorate your frame any way you want.

❊ Tape the photo in place on the back so your face peeks out of the hole.

❊ Make the frame sturdy by gluing another piece of tagboard, the same size as the frame, to the back.

❊ To hang your frame: Tape a short piece of yarn to the back. Loop the yarn over a small nail in the wall.

Fancy Soap

Such a useful gift and so pretty, too!

Bar soap

Christmas stickers

1 bar paraffin (wax)

Pie tin

Small paintbrush

Tissue paper and ribbon

❊ Unwrap the soap. (Allow one bar for every person on your gift list.)

❊ Place a Christmas sticker on top of the soap. You could even create your own stickers using peel-off labels.

❊ Melt the paraffin wax in the pie tin. The pie tin can be placed on top of a saucepan filled with hot water and kept warm on the stove top. Adult help is a must!

❊ Use the paintbrush to coat the sticker and the top surface of the soap with melted wax. A second coat helps seal the sticker for many hand washings.

❊ Once the wax has cooled, wrap your fancy soap in tissue paper and tie with a ribbon. Beautiful!

Key Holder

Everyone needs a place to hang keys. This handsome and practical gift will help your favorite grown-ups be more organized.

Carpenter's wood glue

6 wooden blocks (3 triangles that fit on top of
    3 rectangles or squares)

Acrylic paints and brushes

3 cup hooks

Hanger for picture frames

✳ Glue triangle blocks on top of rectangle or square blocks to make little houses. Glue three houses together to create a mini-neighborhood of homes. Allow to dry overnight (about 8 hours).

✳ Paint the blocks using acrylic paints. It's fun to try to create a replica of your house or the gift recipient's house. Paint your family or a beloved pet in front. Use your imagination!

✳ Along the bottom of the blocks, screw in cup hooks. The hooks will hold the key rings.

✳ Attach a picture-frame hanger on the back so the key holder can hang on a nail.

Warm Wishes Mocha Mix

Hot drink mixes are a delicious way to warm up some-one's winter day. This first recipe is mocha, a blend of chocolate and coffee. The second is for sweet peach tea.

1 cup powdered chocolate-milk mix

3/4 cup powdered nondairy creamer

1/2 cup instant coffee

1/2 teaspoon cinnamon

1/4 teaspoon ground nutmeg

Self-adhesive label

✳ Mix all ingredients in a bowl.

✳ Store in a colorful plastic container.

✳ Decorate a self-adhesive label and apply it to the container with these serving instructions: Add 1 heaping tablespoon of mocha mix to one cup hot water. Stir.

You're-a-Peach Tea Mix

1 cup instant tea mix

1 3-oz. box peach-flavored gelatin

2 cups granulated sugar

Self-adhesive label

✳ Mix all ingredients in a bowl.

✳ Store in a colorful plastic container.

✳ Decorate a self-adhesive label and apply it to the container with these serving instructions: Add 2 tablespoons of tea mix to one cup hot water. Stir.

The Dream Before Christmas

Oliver cracked his eyes open. Christmas morning! He could feel it in his bones. He rolled over and peered into the bunk bed below. The glowworm lamp flickered dimly on the bureau. Oliver could see that Emily's eyes were already wide open.

"Did you sleep?" Emily whispered.

"Not a wink!" Oliver said, rubbing his face. "I never can sleep the night before Christmas."

"Me neither," Emily agreed.

"Howsoever," Oliver said, "I did have a dream that we were opening presents."

"So you did sleep!"

"Did not!" Oliver protested.

"You can't dream and not sleep."

"Well, somehow I managed," Oliver said with a big yawn. "Things like dreaming and not sleeping happen on special nights like Christmas Eve. Don't you remember that poem about visions of sugarplums dancing in the kids' heads? That happened to me last night."

"You had visions of sugarplums?" Emily asked skeptically.

"No. I had visions of custard pies, chocolate éclairs, cherry strudels, and peach cobblers, not to mention assorted tarts. But they were dancing in my head all right."

Like a wise sister, Emily decided to question Oliver's sleep no further. He was terribly silly, but she loved him anyway (well, most of the time).

"What presents were we opening in your dream?" Emily asked.

Oliver sat bolt upright. "I dreamed we got a train set!" He jumped out of bed and went padding into the unlit hall.

"It's not morning yet, Oliver," Emily whispered, and went padding after him. "It's too dark outside."

"It's early morning—can't you tell?" Oliver whispered back. "The dark isn't quite the same."

"Dark is dark, Oliver. Besides, baby Violet is still sleeping."

Oliver hesitated. "But what if nobody bothered to wake us up to open our presents? What if it's so late it's already tomorrow night?"

"What if it's so early that there aren't any presents yet?" Emily countered.

Oliver was weakening. "But, in my dream . . ."

At that moment, there came a cry from the nursery. Both children jumped nervously. "Ha, it *is* morning!" Oliver said triumphantly.

They hurried into the nursery and pulled baby Violet from her crib. "Hush, Violet," Oliver whispered. "We're going downstairs to shake presents. You can come with us if you don't wake Mama and Papa."

Violet sensed that something secret was afoot, so she quieted down after a couple of sniffles. The children carried her to the top of the stairs. The dark tree stretched from the floor below and reached to

the ceiling above their heads. The children could see scarcely anything except the tree's huge shadow. They made their way softly down the stairs . . . step-by-step. Step-by-step. They could feel their hearts beating like big kettledrums. The smell of the tree caused their noses to tingle and their ears to stand straight on end. The suspense was unbearable!

When they got to the bottom step, Oliver hesitated. "My legs feel like oatmeal," he whispered. "I'm so excited, I can hardly stand up."

"Me, too," Emily whispered back. "My legs feel like pats of butter melting on a pancake." She peered into the darkness. "Do you see any packages?"

Suddenly the lights on the tree came on. It happened all at once—a blinding glare of colored lights, tinsel, glass balls, and foil boxes.

"SURPRISE!!!" shouted Mama and Papa. They had been sitting in the parlor waiting for them.

The children were too stunned to utter a word.

Only Violet let out a shrill cry of delight.

"Did you ever think your parents would wake up before you on Christmas Day?" asked Mama.

"Not in a million years!" Emily cried.

"Or a thousand either," added Oliver.

At that moment something stirred at the foot of the tree. There came a low whistle and a puff of steam and a little clickity-clacking noise.

"A train set!!" Oliver whooped.

"A train set!!" Emily screamed. "Your dream came true!"

They danced together in wild circles.

Oliver laughed. "All day long, cabooses will be dancing in my head."

And so they did. Oliver dreamed a waking dream of cabooses, boxcars, and locomotives. And driving the great steam engine was Oliver himself. Every time the whistle blew, it sounded to his ears like *Merry Christmas! Happy New Year!*

Christmas Morning Eyepoppers

It's here at last—the happiest day of the year! The long weeks and months of waiting are finally over.
Here are two tasty breakfast recipes to fortify you for the hard work of unwrapping gifts.
But keep these recipes special—make them only once a year, on Christmas morning.

Reindeer Bread

This bread is as good as sticky cinnamon buns and so easy to make.

4 tubes refrigerated biscuit dough (10 biscuits per tube)

1 3/4 cups granulated sugar

2 1/2 teaspoons ground cinnamon

1/2 cup chopped pecans

3/4 cup (1 1/2 sticks) butter

✳ Preheat oven to 350° F.

✳ Separate biscuits and cut them into quarters. Set aside.

✳ Mix 3/4 cup of the sugar and 1 teaspoon of the cinnamon in a bag. Drop several pieces of biscuit in at a time and shake until coated.

✳ Arrange coated pieces evenly in a decorative cake pan. (A Bundt or angel-food pan is perfect.)

✳ Scatter nuts over biscuit pieces.

✳ Melt butter in saucepan. Add the rest of the sugar (1 cup) and remaining 1 1/2 teaspoons cinnamon. Stir and bring to a boil.

✳ Remove syrup mixture from heat and pour over biscuit pieces.

✳ Bake reindeer bread for 40-45 minutes.

✳ Turn bread out onto a plate. It tastes best if you serve it warm.

Gingerbread Pancakes

If you like gingerbread men, you'll enjoy a stack of these with warm maple syrup.

1 cup flour

1 1/2 teaspoons baking powder

1/2 teaspoon ground ginger

1/2 teaspoon allspice

1/2 teaspoon cinnamon

Dash ground clove

1/2 cup milk

1 large egg, lightly beaten

3 tablespoons molasses

1 tablespoon vegetable oil

Raisins for decoration

✳ Mix all the dry ingredients—flour, baking powder, and spices—together in a medium-sized bowl.

✳ Stir in all the wet ingredients—milk, molasses, vegetable oil, and egg—until just blended. Avoid overbeating or your pancakes may be tough.

✳ Pour small puddles of batter onto a hot buttered skillet. When bubbles begin to appear on the pancakes' top surfaces, decorate each with raisins to form a smiley face. Don't burn your fingers!

✳ Flip pancakes until both sides are golden brown and serve with butter and syrup.

Merry Christmas

M for the Music, merry and clear;

E for the Eve, the crown of the year;

R for the Romping of bright girls and boys;

R for the Reindeer that bring them the toys;

Y for the Yule log softly aglow.

C for the Cold of the sky and the snow;

H for the Hearth where they hang up the hose;

R for the Reels which the old folks propose;

I for the Icicles seen through the pane;

S for the Sleigh bells, with tinkling refrain;

T for the Tree with gifts all abloom;

M for the Mistletoe hung in the room;

A for the Anthems we all love to hear;

S for St. Nicholas—joy of the year!

—FROM ST. NICHOLAS MAGAZINE, JANUARY 1897